FOLLOW THE DREAM

by Peter Sis

DRAGONFLY BOOKS™

Alfred A. Knopf, New York

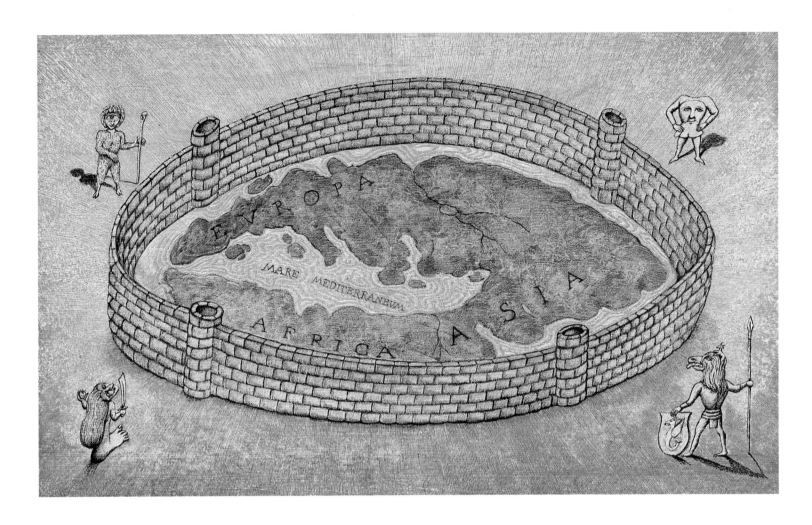

DRAGONFLY BOOKS PUBLISHED BY ALFRED A. KNOPF, INC.

Copyright © 1991 Peter Sis

http://www.randomhouse.com/

Library of Congress Cataloging-in-Publication Data
Sis, Peter.
Follow the dream : the story of Christopher Columbus / by Peter Sis
p. cm.
Summary: In a pictorial retelling, Christopher Columbus overcomes a number of obstacles to fulfill his dream of sailing west to find a new route to the Orient.
ISBN 0-679-80628-8 (trade) — ISBN 0-679-90628-2 (lib. bdg.) —ISBN 0-679-88088-7 (pbk.)
1. Columbus, Christopher—Juvenile literature. 2. Explorers—America—Biography—Juvenile literature.
3. Explorers—Spain—Biography—Juvenile literature. 4. America—Discovery and exploration—Spanish—Juvenile literature. [1. Columbus, Christopher. 2. Explorers.] I. Title.
E111.S56 1991 970.01'5 [E]—dc20 93-12341
[B] [92] 90-45276
First Dragonfly Books edition: September 1996
Printed in the United States of America
10 9 8 7 6 5 4 3 2

A Note to the Reader:

When I came to America in 1982, all I knew about Christopher Columbus was that he had sailed the ocean blue in 1492. Then I read many books about him and studied maps that he himself might have looked at. Some of them showed Europe surrounded by high walls, with monsters standing guard beyond—like the map I have drawn on the opposite page.

Columbus didn't let the walls hold him back. For him, the outside world was not to be feared but *explored*. And so he followed his dream. He wrote in his diary:

> *I went sailing upon the sea and have*
> *continued to this day, which very*
> *occupation inclines all who follow it*
> *to wish to learn the secrets of the world.*

Since I, too, grew up in a country surrounded by a "wall," known as the Iron Curtain, I was inspired to make this book, which I finished with the help of Frances Foster and Terry Lajtha in time for the 500th anniversary of Christopher Columbus's voyage.

Peter Sis

 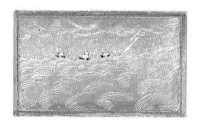 

Over 500 years ago in the city of Genoa, in Italy,

a little boy was born. His name was Christopher
Columbus.

It was expected that Christopher would grow up to be a weaver, like his father.

But Christopher Columbus had his own ideas about his
future.

He dreamed of the faraway places and people he read
about in *The Travels of Marco Polo.*

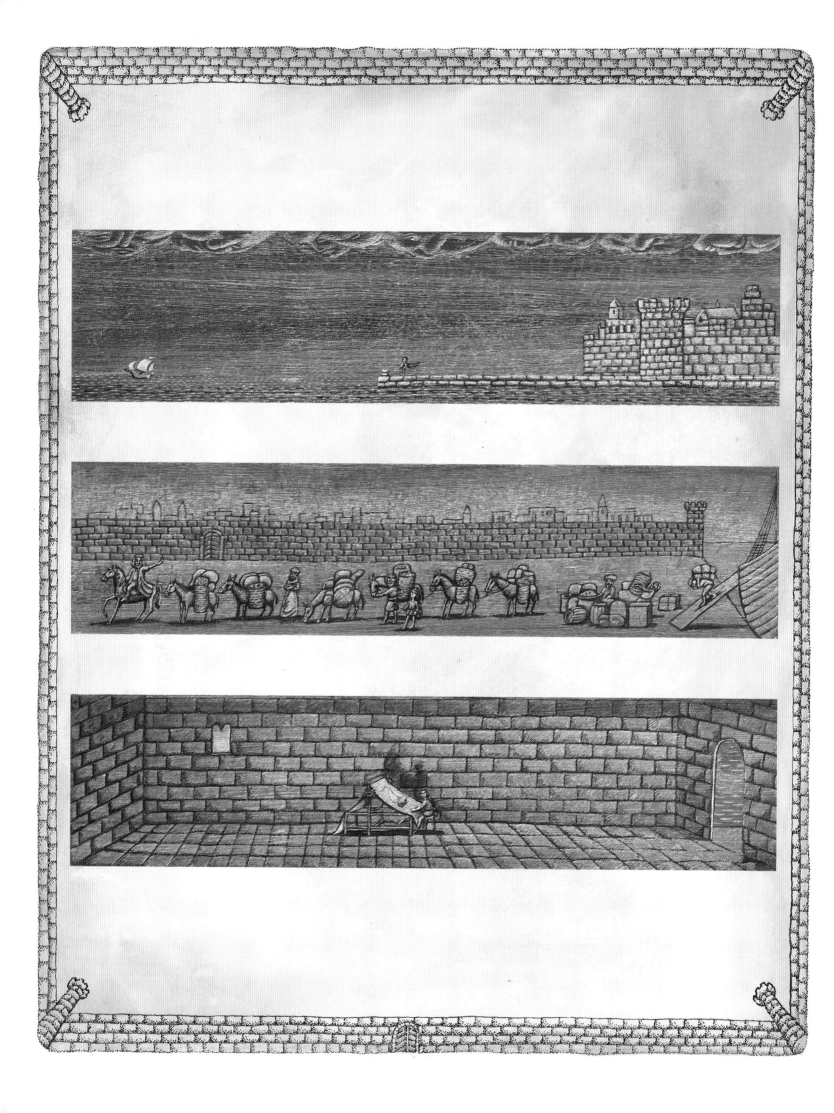

He watched the ships in the harbor of Genoa and listened to the merchants and sailors as they unloaded their cargoes of exotic goods and spices brought from the Orient. And he kept weaving dreams of adventure and discovery.

As the years went by, Christopher Columbus formed a plan. He would reach the Orient by a new route. Rather than traveling east over a thousand miles of difficult terrain, he would sail west, across the Atlantic Ocean.

Fulfilling his dream was not easy. He had to become an expert sailor and had to learn how to read maps and the stars for navigation.

He traveled throughout the Mediterranean and Europe,
looking for a sponsor to provide him with the ships,
supplies, and crew he would need for the long journey west.

Everyone thought Columbus's plan was too risky, or too
expensive, or just impossible. But Columbus always
expected that someday he would be granted his ships. He
approached the King and Queen of Spain.

King Ferdinand and Queen Isabella listened quietly to
Christopher Columbus, though his ideas about the world
were so different from those of their advisers. They told
him no.

Columbus had a second audience with the King and
Queen, but it went no better than the first. His proposal to
find a new trade route to the Orient by sailing west was
rejected once more.

Six years later, Christopher Columbus was still the only
one to believe that land lay to the west, across the ocean,
and that riches would be found there.

But now Queen Isabella was intrigued. She offered the King her jewels as a token of her faith in Columbus's plan. Persuaded by his wife's conviction, the King decided to take a chance. He would provide Christopher Columbus with three ships and a crew of ninety men.

The ships were stocked with food and water and goods
for trading.

Six months later, on August 3, 1492, the *Niña*, the *Pinta*, and the *Santa María* set sail from Palos, Spain.

The three ships headed west, taking advantage of the trade winds, which Columbus hoped would carry them directly to their destination. The sea was calm, and at first it seemed the journey would be easy.

But from the beginning the crew was uneasy. The endless expanse of sea, with its unfamiliar birds and fish and seaweed, frightened them. They wanted to turn back. Columbus was determined to keep sailing west.

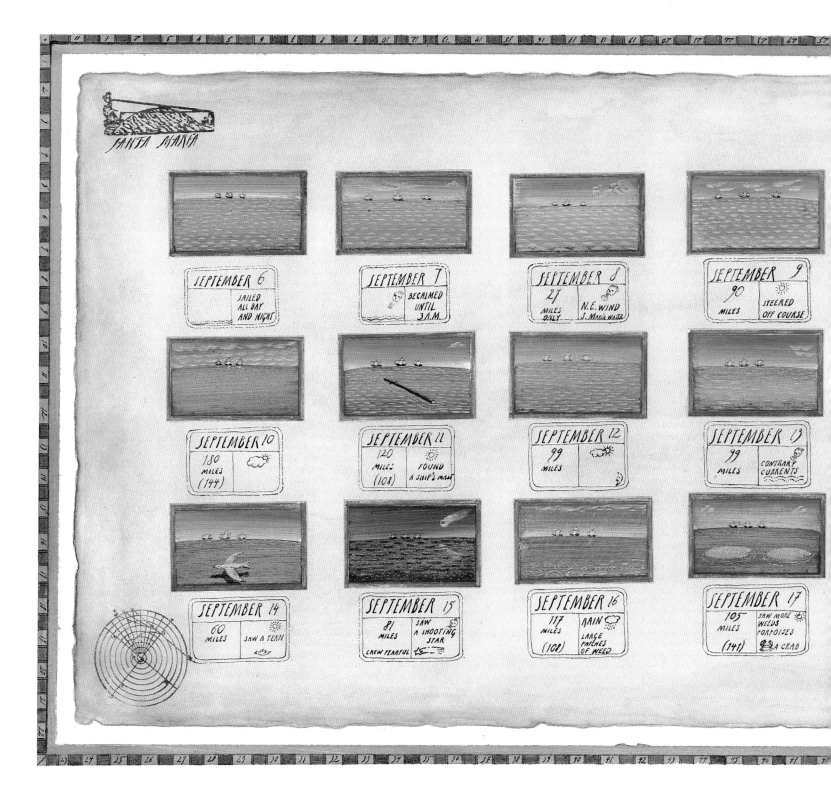

In his cabin on the *Santa María,* Columbus kept the record of the voyage in the ship's log. But he actually kept two logs. In one, he shortened the distances to reassure the rebellious crew.

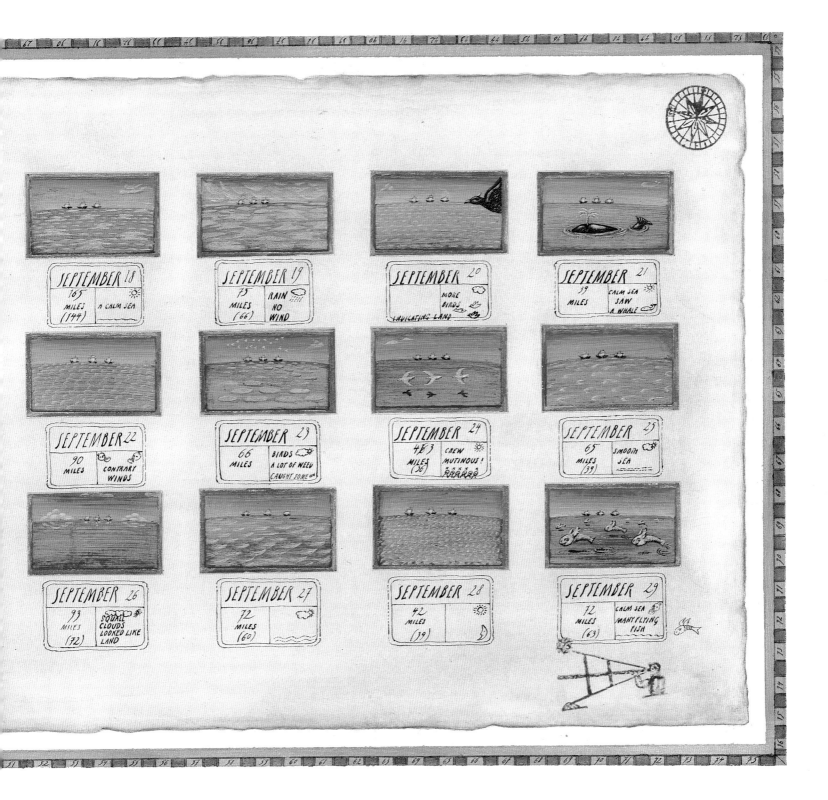

Day after day, through all kinds of weather, the three
ships continued on their westward course.

Then, on the seventy-first day, a little piece of land
appeared on the horizon.

Columbus assumed it was part of Japan.

On October 12, 1492, just after midday, Christopher Columbus landed on a beach of white coral, claimed the land for the King and Queen of Spain, knelt and gave thanks to God, and expected to see the treasures of the Orient. . . .

Today we know that what Christopher Columbus found was not a new route to the Orient but a new continent. Columbus, however, never really knew that he had reached "America."

Peter Sis came to America from Czechoslovakia in 1982, and in 1989 became a U.S. citizen. He was inspired by his own discovery of a new world to think about Christopher Columbus and that most famous voyage of exploration. Drawing upon fifteenth-century maps, *The Travels of Marco Polo*, and contemporary sources, he has imagined what the world must have been like for a boy growing up in Genoa, Italy, at a time when most people thought that nothing but endless sea lay to the west of Europe.

Peter Sis studied painting and filmmaking at the Academy of Applied Arts in Prague and at the Royal College of Art in London. He has written and illustrated many books for children, among them *Rainbow Rhino*. He now lives in New York City.